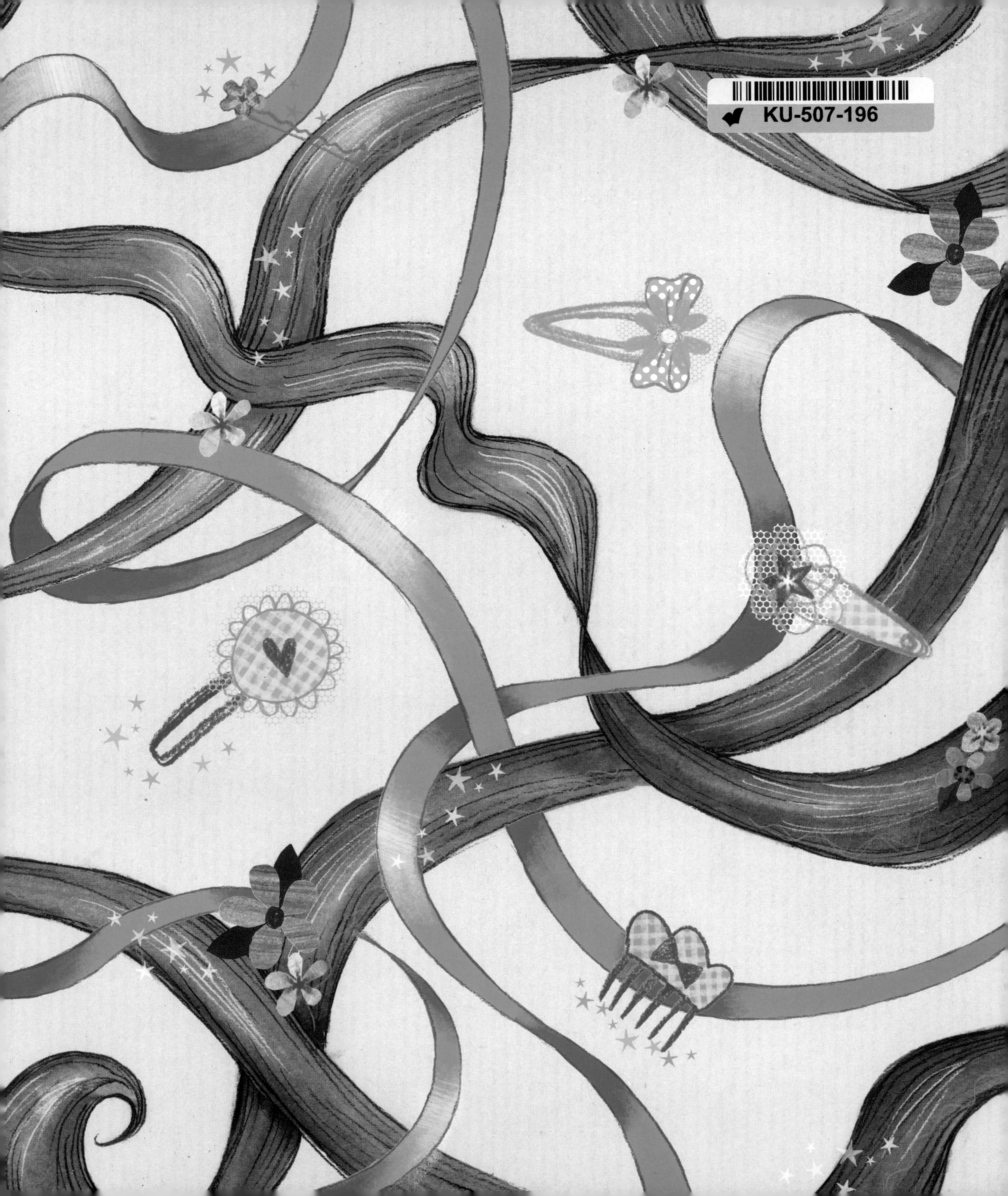

For Ada ~ my beautiful baby with rosy-gold hair ~ S S

For Elodie with love ~ L S

LITTLE TIGER PRESS LTD,
an imprint of the Little Tiger Group
1 Coda Studios, 189 Munster Road,
London SW6 6AW
www.littletiger.co.uk

First published in Great Britain 2019
This edition published 2019

A CIP catalogue record for this book is
available from the British Library

ISBN 978-1-78881-368-6
LTP/1400/2906/0819 • Printed in China
2 4 6 8 10 9 7 5 3

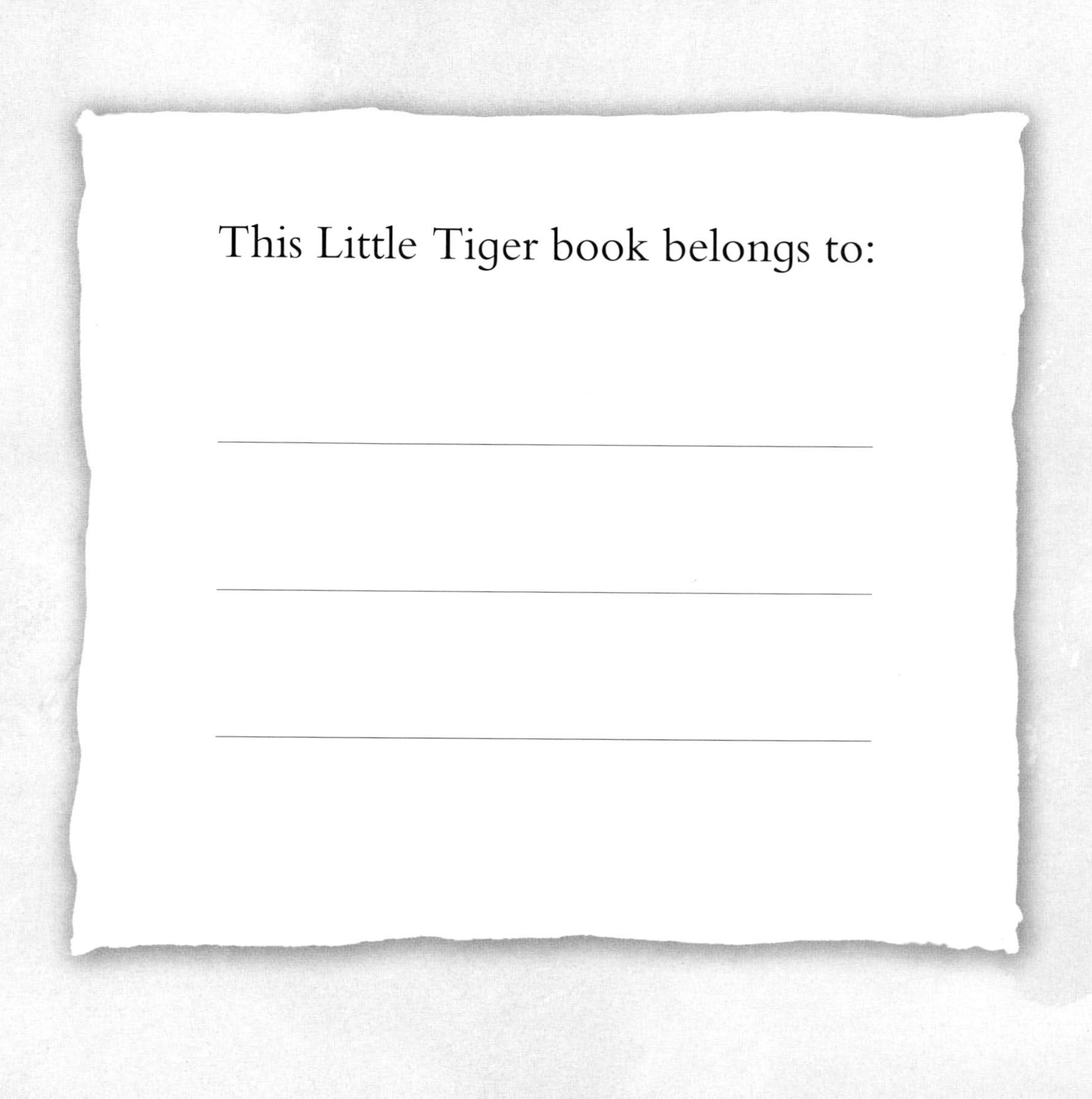
This Little Tiger book belongs to:

FAIRYTALE CLASSICS

Rapunzel

Stephanie Stansbie
Loretta Schauer

Bessie and Bert Greensmith loved each other very much. But something was missing. And that something was a child.

"Why so glum, precious one?" Bert asked one day.

"I love you, Bert," Bessie said. "But I'd really like a baby."

Bert thought for a while. "Our neighbour's garden is packed with delicious vegetables. Maybe they'd help us have a child. You know what they say:

Eat your greens – they'll make you great.
So pile some veg on every plate!"

"Don't go next door," Bessie pleaded. "That old lady's a bit of a witch."

But Bert wanted a child as much as his wife. So one moonlit night, he . . .

picked a pepper . . .

lopped a lettuce . . .

and bagged some beetroot!

And guess what? The following year, Bessie and Bert had a bouncing baby girl.

But that night something terrible happened.
The witch from next door snuck into the house
and took the baby away.
"Steal from me and I'll steal from you!"
she cackled (as witches do).

Then she built a dingy, doorless tower
deep in the darkest wood and hid
Rapunzel inside.

Rapunzel was lonely of course. But she also grew up to be very inventive.

She had to be, locked in a tower all day!

She built herself a model railway, a unicycle, even a telescope, and made up **hundreds** of songs.

When the witch came to the tower,
she stood at the bottom and yelled:
"Rapunzel, Rapunzel, let down your hair!"

Rapunzel's rosy-gold hair had grown
so long, all the witch had to do was
clamber up. It was very uncomfortable.
But Rapunzel was used to it.

"When can I go out and explore?" she asked every single day.

But the witch always had the same answer: "The world is full of rascals and robbers. They'll steal the hair off your head."

One day, a prince was hunting in the woods, when he heard Rapunzel's voice.

"What an incredible singer," he thought, gazing up at the tower. *"But how do I get up there?"*

Just then he heard the witch shuffling along the path, and he dived into a bush.

When the witch started scaling Rapunzel's lustrous locks, the prince was flabbergasted. "*Now I've seen everything!*" he thought.

Once the witch had left,
the prince called up:
"Rapunzel, Rapunzel,
let down your hair!"

“Who are you?” Rapunzel yelped, when she saw the prince at her window.

“I’m Freddie,” said Prince Freddie. “Can I come in?”

“Depends if you’re going to steal something,” Rapunzel said. “I’m a black belt in karate, you know – self-taught!”

But Rapunzel decided to show him all the things she’d made.

They talked and talked. Freddie was funny and he knew SO much stuff.

But then the witch came back.

Freddie held out his hand to the old lady.

"I'd like to take Rapunzel to the palace," he said.

The witch's face was dangerous and dark.

"Steal from me and I'll steal from you," she hissed.

Then
she
hurled
him
out
of
the
tower!

"You'll never leave this place," the witch snarled. "You're mine." And she jumped out of the window, yanking hard at Rapunzel's locks.

"*Harrumph! Nobody owns me*," thought Rapunzel. Then she cut off her rosy-gold hair, tied it to the window and sailed down.

When Rapunzel found Freddie, he was battered and blind. “I’m so sorry,” she sniffed, wiping her eyes.

“It’s not your fault,” Freddie smiled. “Please don’t cry.”

But Rapunzel's tears
were like magic.

Freddie blinked.
He could see again!

Back at the palace, Freddie made Rapunzel his **Chief Inventor** and they became firm friends.

Rapunzel built all sorts of cool things for the kingdom – even a harvesting machine. Then she offered free vegetables to everyone in the land. And guess what?

She gave the witch the job of giving out the greens!

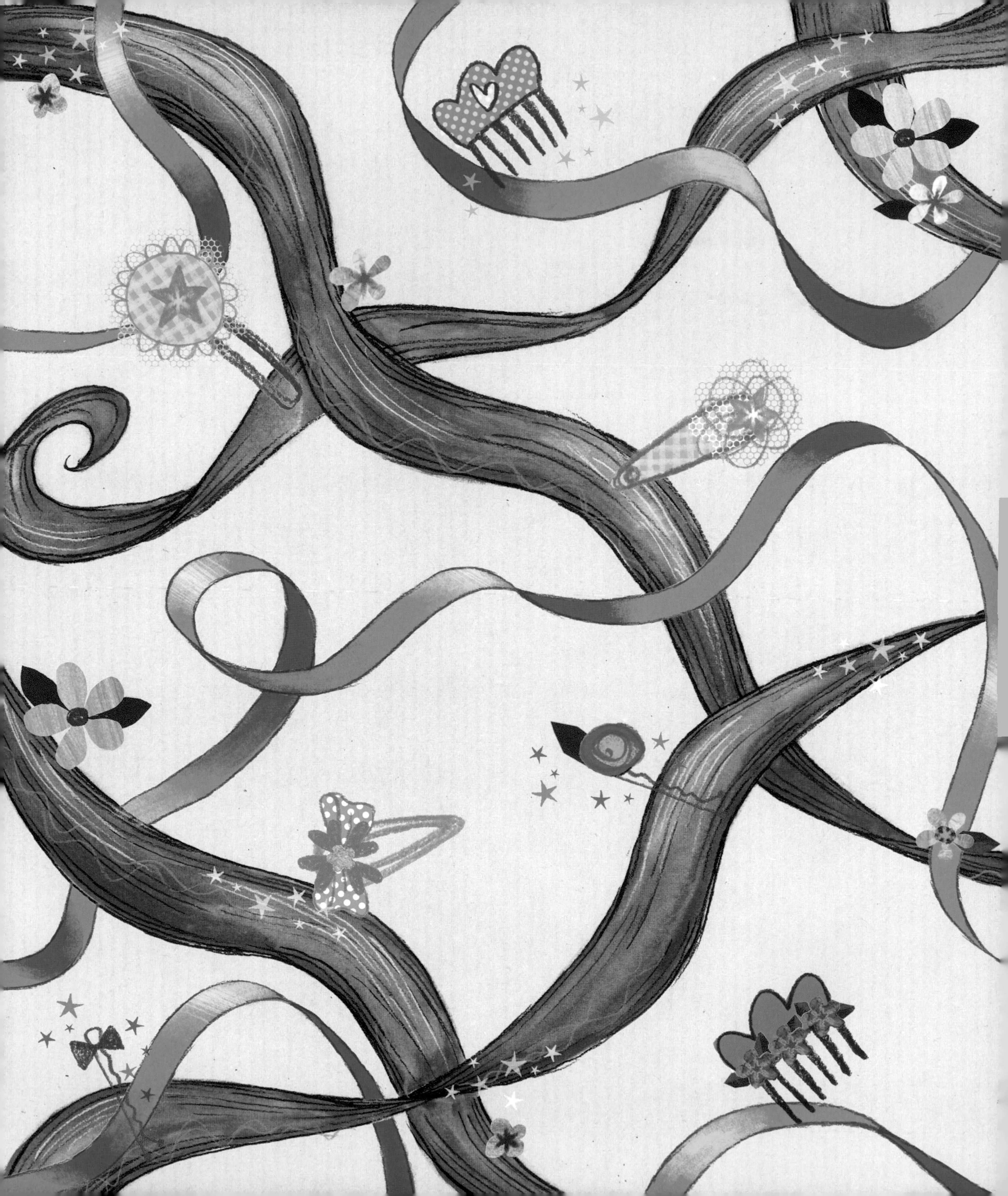